T0198991

I Do Believe

By
Margaret Christie

Print information available on the last page

Rev. date: 11/07/2019

To order additional copies of this book, contact:
Xlibris
1-888-795-4274
www.Xlibris.com
Orders@Xlibris.com

ACKNOWLEDGEMENT

In grateful appreciation to Kimberly and Michael Meredith for helping me and supporting me in getting this book published. Thank you so much! Blessings to you both.

Ten year old Jamie Patterson looked out the window at the Autumn sunset. He could see the sky splashed with crimson red and gold. He ran a hand through his matching sky red hair and sighed. His chest felt tight and his heart was sad. Jamie's mom, Mary, was in the hospital bed behind him. Her face was pale and her eyes were red and swollen. He saw a reflection in the window of someone coming into the room. He turned around and faced the nurse Martha. She was carrying tray with medication and a cup of water. Her nurse's tunic had butterflies that seemed to fly as she moved toward the bed. This reminded Jamie of the stories about angels his mother so often told to him.

Martha looked at Jamie and spoke softly, "Where is your Dad?" Jamie responded that his Dad was down the hall talking to Dr. Martin. They were gone for a long time.

"I hope they come back soon," said Martha. "Visiting hours are almost over." Jamie turned toward the doorway and saw his father come back into the room. He looked exhausted. He was running his hand nervously through his dark red hair. Everyone said that Jamie resembled his Dad in so many ways.

"I'm glad I was able to get back in time to say goodnight to your Mom before we leave." He looked at his wife, Mary, lying there, bent over, kissed her on the forehead and whispered. "Goodnight my Honey."

"Goodnight Mom, I love you," Jamie said. Jamie turned towards his Dad so Mary would not see his face. He swallowed hard and blinked back his tears.

Jamie shoved his hands into his pants pockets. He and his Dad walked to the elevators. They noticed a chapel on the right side.

Rob said, "Let's stop in here for a moment." They sat down in a rear pew. covering his face and quietly whispering to himself. "Oh God, what is going to happen?" he thought. "My Faith isn't strong. I don't know what to do, think or believe. What can I say to Jamie?" He became lost in thought.

"Dad, will mom be all right?" Jamie asked.

"Well son, from what the doctor told me... it's not good. She has a rare strain of cancer in the blood. It is called Leukemia. She may not be with us much longer."

Jamie looked at his Dad. His face was suddenly pale. Tears formed in his eyes and a few drops fell streaking his face.

Jamie said, "Mom talked to me about Jesus and guardian angels." He wiped his eyes "We all have a guardian angel." Rob didn't know what to say. He himself had been questioning his Faith for some time even before Mary's diagnosis of Leukemia. He was not as close to God like Mary. She worked on Sundays as a Religion teacher. She taught her son and the other children about Jesus, the Blessed Mother, and angels. These angels she called God's messengers.

Rob swallowed hard and then spoke to Jamie.

"We have to go now. We're going to your Aunt Marjorie's and Uncle Jim's so you can visit your cousin Billy. We'll have a late supper there." Marjorie was Mary's sister. She and her husband Jim, and cousin Billy often got together. They all lived a few blocks from each other and the boys went to the same school.

Jamie remembered when he had come home from school the previous week. His mom had made freshly baked chocolate chip/walnut cookies and milk. They were his favorite snack. She had dropped the glass of milk. It was on the floor mixed with the glass fragments surrounding her feet.

Jamie was shocked at the scene before him. He remembered that frightened look on her face as she had cut herself badly picking up the broken glass. One second she was standing up; the next second she had fainted to the floor. Jamie ran to the phone to call 911. The paramedics had trouble reviving her and stopping the blood flow from her hand.

The paramedics told Jamie they would have to take her to the nearby Emergency Room at Good Shepherd Hospital. Jamie hurried to reach his father on his cell phone. He explained what happened. He then called Aunt Marjorie and asked her take them to the hospital. By the time they arrived at the hospital, Mary was already in surgery. They were praying for the best.

A few days later...Rob and Jamie were in the hospital room. Her eyes were closed. Suddenly her eyes opened and she spoke. "Rob...Jamie, I am so glad you both came."

Rob asked Dr. Martin, "How much time does she have?"

Dr. Martin replied sadly, "Any time now. We're trying to make her as comfortable as possible. Be with her as much as you can." Mary's eyelids fluttered suddenly. Her hazel eyes shimmered with a golden glow. She looked at them and spoke. She gave a faint smile trying to keep her eyes open.

"Jamie do you remember what I told you about guardian angels? Rob you've been so good to me. I love you both." Her voice faded out and then such a glow came upon her face. Her eyes closed and then she was gone.

"Oh, God no!" Rob choked out the words. "I don't know how I can cope." He thought, "What about Jamie? I don't know what to say to Jamie...Oh Mary."

"Dad?" Tears were running down Jamie's face. Rob could barely speak. Dr. Martin led them out to the waiting area. He told them what they needed to do. Jamie sat down and sobbed. Rob called his sister-in-law, Marjorie, and told her about Mary's passing. Then he told Jamie they were going to Aunt Marjorie's and Uncle Jim's place to discuss funeral arrangements.

The following week the whole family drove in Rob's van to Mount Calvary cemetery. Suddenly a sunbeam illuminated the rear of the hearse ahead of them. Jamie asked if anyone saw the same thing he did.

Aunt Marjorie replied, "Yes, I saw the light. "It was nice to see the sun for a short while," She had a hat on with a couple of feathers that fluttered. She turned toward the back of the car to speak to Jamie.

Jamie suddenly thought about what he had seen. "Did I see angel feathers?" Jamie whispered. "I thought I saw something in the light. A figure was sitting on the back of the hearse!"

Rob looked at Jamie, "I did see the light. Was there something else?" It was hard for Rob to talk to Jamie since Mary's passing. He felt such a loss. It was still hard for him to reach out to Jamie.

People pulled up behind them and they walked up to the grave site. Jamie looked up at the cloudy sky. Another sunbeam came down to the grave and shimmered. There was something about the sunbeam. A winged figure formed overhead. Then it disappeared. Jamie caught his breath.

"Dad, did you see the same thing I did? A light over the coffin."

"Yes, I did." Rob replied, "Did you see anything else?"

"No." Jamie said. He was puzzled. "Could it have been an angel?" Once again Jamie remembered what his mom had said about guardian angels.

Later that evening Jamie was in his bedroom. A single soft light was lit on the bedside table and Jamie was looking out the window at the stars.

"Oh God," he prayed and then started to cry. A soft glow reflected in the window. It came from behind Jamie. He turned around to see a golden light. An angel appeared dressed in a flowing white robe. He had on a brown belt with a gold buckle around his waist. He was standing on the bed. The wings fluttered slightly and then stilled.

"Don't be afraid Jamie," the angel said. "I'm your guardian angel, Jeffrey."

"My guardian angel?" Jamie was startled at what he was seeing and hearing.

"I didn't know our guardian angels had names."

"Yes!" said the angel. "Not many people do know, but we most certainly do . God heard your prayer and asked me to talk to you. He knows you miss your Mom. He wants me to help you realize what happened to her."

"Jamie, who are you taking to?" Rob asked as he walked in the room and saw the angel. Then he remembered the sunbeam on the hearse, and the light at the cemetery.

"Were you at the cemetery?" Rob and Jamie said in unison.

"No." said Jeffrey, "that was the angel which guided your Mom to heaven to be with God. She is out of pain and free now."

"Will I be able to see her again?" Jamie asked Jeffrey

Jeffrey replied, "You still have a long time here with your Dad." Jeffrey continued. "Your mother hoped your dad would believe too! God loves both of you more than you know. Rob, here is your guardian angel, Max. He will be beside you at all times."

The second angel appeared dressed just like Jeffrey, but he did not speak.

He nodded to Rob in acknowledgement.

"We will be invisible but always at your side throughout your lives." Jeffrey and Max smiled and then they disappeared. Jamie and his dad looked at each other in wonder. Relief and peace washed over them.

"Yes." Rob said in awe to Jamie. "Now I do believe in what your mom said about guardian angels, and in God who created them. How can I not believe? This visitation has wiped away any doubt." Jamie flung himself into his Dad's arms. He hugged him tightly, gazed up at his Dad and smiled.

Printed in the United States
By Bookmasters